JUDY MOODY AND FRIENDS

Stink Moody
in Master of Disaster

Megan McDonald

illustrated by Erwin Madrid
based on the characters
created by Peter H. Reynolds

CANDLEWICK PRESS

For Heather McGee, Rachel Smith,
Lisa Rudden, and Pam Consolazio

M. M.

For my brother, Edward, and
sister-in-law, Vallejule

E. M.

Text copyright © 2015 by Megan McDonald
Illustrations copyright © 2015 by Peter H. Reynolds
Judy Moody font copyright © 2003 by Peter H. Reynolds

Judy Moody®. Judy Moody is a registered trademark of Candlewick Press, Inc.
Stink®. Stink is a registered trademark of Candlewick Press, Inc.

First edition 2015

Library of Congress Catalog Card Number 2013957338
ISBN 978-0-7636-7218-8 (hardcover)
ISBN 978-0-7636-7447-2 (paperback)

15 16 17 18 19 CCP 10 9 8 7 6 5 4 3 2

Printed in Shenzhen, Guangdong, China

This book was typeset in ITC Stone Informal.
The illustrations were created digitally.

Candlewick Press
99 Dover Street
Somerville, Massachusetts 02144

visit us at www.candlewick.com

CONTENTS

CHAPTER 1
The Sherlock-Holmes Comet

Judy and Stink were sleeping out in the backyard. Judy and Stink were stargazing. Judy and Stink were searching the sky for comet P/2015 OZ4. The Sherman-Holm comet. Stink called it the Sherlock-Holmes comet.

The night sky looked like the *Starry Night* painting, only better. "No blinking, Stink," Judy told him.

"A comet is a once-in-a-lifetime thing. No way would you want to miss it."

Stink tried not to blink. But thinking about blinking just made him blinkier.

"Sure is dark out here," said Stink.

"That's because it's nighttime, Stink."

"Sure is quiet out here," said Stink.

"That's because it's nighttime, Stink."

3

Judy pointed to a band of stars that looked like a giant brushstroke across the sky. "That's the Milky Way," said Judy.

"Hey! There's the Big Dipper. And the Little Dipper. And the Medium Dipper."

"And there's Wynken, Blynken, and Nod," said Judy.

"For real?" asked Stink.

"Gotcha!" said Judy, laughing herself silly.

It was dark for a long time. It was quiet for a long time.

"They should call this star-*waiting*," said Stink.

"Good things come to those who wait, Stink."

"Says who?"

"Abe Lincoln. The ketchup bottle. Mom and Dad."

While he waited, Stink dumped out his backpack. "Star book. Star map. Star finder. Flashlight. Toilet-paper-tube telescope, and . . . my Star Talker DL7."

Stink pressed a button.

"*The full moon in March is called a Worm Moon.*"

Stink pressed the button again.

"*A star in Draco, the Dragon, was used by ancient Egyptians to build pyramids.*"

Stink pressed the button again.

"*The full moon in March is called a Worm Moon.*"

Stink pressed the button again.

"*The full moon in March is called a Worm Moon.*"

Judy put her hands over her ears. "Make that thing stop! All you need for stargazing is your eyes, Stink. And a little P and Q."

"P and Q?"

"Peace and quiet."

Stink opened his *Big Head Book of Stars.* Stink held his star map up to the sky. He turned it this way and that.

Judy watched the twinkling stars in the velvet sky and waited.

Stink spun his star finder to August.

Stink squinted one eye and looked through his toilet-paper-tube telescope.

Stink studied his star map. He found the Eagle,

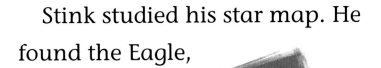

Pegasus,

and Draco
on the map.

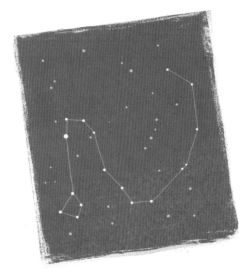

11

Judy studied the night sky. She found the Swan, the tail of Scorpius, and the Summer Triangle in the sky. Then she saw . . . a flash of light. A giant ball of fire streaked across the inky sky faster than a wink! Faster than a blink.

Judy jumped up. "Stink? Did you . . . did you see that?"

Stink looked up from his map. "See what?"

"The comet! I think Sherlock-Holmes just flew across the sky!"

"I missed it?" Stink wailed. "Wait. What did it look like?"

"Like a red-hot freaky fireball streaking across the sky. Like Fourth of July fireworks. Like five thousand shooting stars."

"No way did you see a comet," said Stink. "Comets are made of ice, not fire. They don't streak across the sky. And a comet has a tail. Did it have a tail?"

Judy shrugged.

"It was probably just a shooting star or a meteor or a fireball or a supernova."

"Or a UFO!" Judy teased.

"Whatever it was, maybe it'll go by again!" Stink said hopefully.

"It will," said Judy. "In about a hundred years."

"A hundred years! I can't wait till I'm a hundred and seven!"

Judy got an idea. "Stink, I know how you can see a comet." She crawled inside the T. P. Club tent. "Don't come in until I say so."

Stink waited for what felt like a hundred and seven years. "Can I come in yet?"

"Not yet."

Stink itched and scratched and waited. "Now?"

"Not yet."

"How about now?"

"No!"

"Did you know the full moon in March is called a Worm Moon?" Stink asked.

Silence.

"There sure is a lot of peace and quiet out here," said Stink.

"You can come in now," said Judy.

Finally! Stink crawled into the tent. The inside was covered with stars— glow-in-the-dark star stickers.

"Wow!" Stink gazed up at his own small sky. "There's the Big Dipper! And the Little Dipper. Even the Medium Dipper!"

Judy pointed to a three-star cluster.

"This is Wynken, Blynken, and Nod.
And that's not all," said Judy. She turned
on not one but two flashlights. One
made a fuzzy ball on the tent sky. She
held the other flashlight at an angle to
make a tail.

"It's a comet!" said Stink. "The
Sherlock-Holmes comet!"

17

When Judy's arms got tired, she turned off the flashlights and crawled inside her sleeping bag. "Show's over. I'm going to bed."

"I didn't get to see the real comet," said Stink, "but I got the next best thing. My own private galaxy. Thanks, Judy."

"Mm-hmm," said a sleepy Judy.

Stink opened the tent flap to peek at the real sky one last time. The stars twinkled like glitter. All of a sudden, a star streaked across the sky.

"A shooting star!" said Stink. "I saw one! For real!"

"Make a wish," mumbled Judy.

Stink closed his eyes and made a wish.

That night, Stink and Judy went to
the Land of Nod under the winking,
blinking stars. If Stink's wish came
true, they would be doing the exact
same thing in another hundred years.

CHAPTER 2
Master of Disaster

Stink raced home from Saturday Science Club. "The sky is falling! The sky is falling!"

Judy looked up from her ant habitat. "Slow down, Chicken Little," said Judy. "What are you saying?"

"The asteroids are coming! The asteroids are coming! I just found out that a giant meteorite landed in

Russia. No lie. And an even bigger one might be headed for Earth."

"Don't worry, Stink. Dad says tons of space junk hits Earth every day."

"*Don't worry?* Tell that to the dinosaurs. There could be a rock out there with *your* name on it. It could be speeding toward Earth right now, going sixty miles per second. *Disaster*oid!"

Judy watched an ant dig a tunnel.

"How can you think about ants at a time like this?" Stink cried. "Any minute you could be squashed like a pancake. Or squished right down to the size of . . . an ant!"

"Ooh, I could be a yellow crazy ant," said Judy. "And you could be an odorous ant. Odorous ants smell like rotting coconuts when you squish them."

"Get serious," said Stink.

"Stink, if an asteroid hits Earth—"

"You said *if*. But it's not *if*, Judy. It's *when*."

"What can *I* do about it?" asked Judy.

"You can build a net the size of Virginia to catch the asteroid. You can invent an anti-asteroid Blast-o-Matic machine to destroy it before it reaches us. *Blaster*oid!"

"That sounds too much like homework," said Judy.

"*I'm* going to make an asteroid-proof bunker in the basement."

"You hate the basement," said Judy. "Dark. Scary. Spiders."

"I'd rather be bitten by ten hundred spiders than squished to the size of a coconut ant by a killer asteroid."

Stink put on his bike helmet, water wings, and knee pads. He made himself an aluminum-foil cape. *Asteroid Boy!* Asteroid Boy would protect Earth from killer asteroids!

Stink carried a blanket, a flashlight, and a light saber down to the basement. He carried Toady the toad and Astro the guinea pig to the basement. He carried half his room to the basement. He even took the toaster to the basement.

"Mom! Dad!" called Judy. "Stink just moved into the basement."

"He hates the basement," said Mom.

"That's what I said," said Judy.

"Why the basement?" asked Dad.

"To hide from killer asteroids," said Judy. "They're speeding toward Earth this very second."

"Tons of space junk hits Earth every day," said Dad.

"That's what I said you said," said Judy.

"He'll change his mind at the first sign of a spider," said Mom.

"He'll change his mind as soon as it gets dark," said Dad.

Judy and Mouse the cat tiptoed down the stairs to the stinky basement. Stink had built a fort out of boxes and boards, chairs and crates.

"Like my bunker?" Stink asked.
Before Judy could answer, a loud
roaring sound came from outside.
"Did you hear that? A sonic boom!"

"Lawn mower," said Judy.

Next they heard a whooshing
sound.

ASTEROID-FREE
ZONE

"Did you hear that?" said Stink. "A space storm!"

"Washing machine," said Judy.

Stink heard a crash like breaking glass.

"It's here!" Stink cried. "The asteroid has landed!"

"That was Dad. Doing dishes again," said Judy.

"Do you feel hot?" Stink asked. "I feel hot." He peered out the window. "Did the house just shake? Is that a radioactive glow?"

Just then, the lights went out. The basement went dark. Dark as an eclipse. Dark as a black hole.

"This is it! Killer asteroid hits Earth and takes out power grid!" Stink threw on a pair of goggles, grabbed his light saber, and yelled, "Never fear! Asteroid Boy is here!" He pointed to the toaster, which was covered with magnets. "Judy, activate the Anti-Asteroid Magnetic-Repulsion Device!"

"Stink, I think *you're* the asteroid. You have too much stuff plugged in down here. You blew a fuse. Dad's going to blow a fuse, too."

"But . . . we're alive!" said Stink. He fell to his knees in relief. "We survived a giant ball of rock, metal, and dust crashing into Earth at sixty thousand miles per second."

Judy sniffed the air. "I don't smell rotting coconuts. So I guess we didn't get squashed like ants."

Stink ran outside. Judy ran after him.

Stink peered up at the sky with his asteroid-proof X-ray-vision goggles. Stink peered up into the trees. Stink peered down at the grass.

"I need proof," said Stink. "Proof that I survived an asteroid hitting Earth faster than a speeding bullet."

"You're proof, Stink. I'm proof. See? We're not as flat as pancakes."

"Pancakes! That reminds me. I'm hungry."

"Surviving an asteroid attack will do that," said Judy. "Let's ask Mom if she'll make us silver-dollar pancakes."

"*When,*" said Stink.

"Huh?"

"Not *if. When.* Ask Mom *when* she's going to make us pancakes."

"Stink, you are the Master of Disaster!" said Judy. "If an asteroid ever hits Earth, I'm calling Asteroid Boy."

"Not *if*," said Asteroid Boy, grinning ear to ear. "*When.*"

CHAPTER 3
Albert Einstink

PLOP! A big fat envelope landed on the Moodys' front step.

"It's for me!" said Stink.

"It's for me!" said Judy.

"But it has *my* name on it," said Stink.

Judy stared at the big fat envelope. It was not her mail-order ants.

Stink grabbed the envelope and

tore it open. "It's from the way-official Name-That-Star Company."

"Name-the-What?"

"Name-That-Star. I'm going to have a star named after me."

"Stink, there are a million, billion stars in the galaxy. I don't think they're going to name one for you."

"Yah-huh." He held up the papers. "It's all right here in my star-naming kit. There's a way-official certificate.

Way-official instructions.

And a real-and-actual
photo of my very own
star."

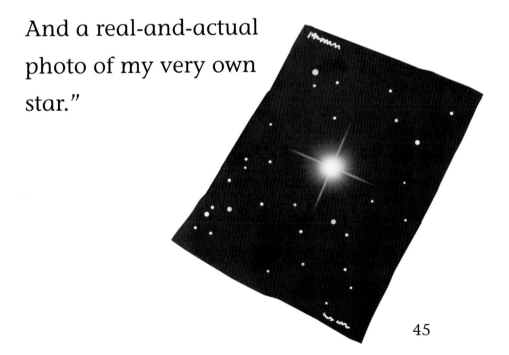

Judy studied the star photo. "Huh. What are you going to name it? *Stink Star?*" She cracked up.

Stink's jaw dropped. "Oh, no," he moaned. "I never thought of that. The Stink Star is not a very good name for a star."

"Use your real name. Call it the James Star."

"*James* is not special enough for a star. There are three Jameses in my second-grade class!"

Judy picked up her Grouchy pencil. "I'll help you. You make a list of names, and I'll make a list of names. Then you'll have tons of names to choose from."

Stink thought and thought. Stink chewed his pencil.

Judy scribbled on her list. "Stella? Stellina? Starla?" she read.

"No girl names," said Stink.

"Orion? Sirius? Hercules?"

"Taken," said Stink.

"Balthazar?"

"Balthazar Moody," said Stink. "Maybe."

"Let's hear some names on your list," said Judy.

"Batman? Superman? Plutoman?"

"Superman Moody? No way. There's kryptonite in outer space, you know. Your star would get clobbered."

"Spike? Dracula? Godzilla?" Stink asked.

"Dracula Moody. I like it!" said Judy. "But it would starve up there."

Stink got out the *Big Head Book of Baby Names.* "Maybe I'll find a name in here!" He opened to the *A*'s. "Abner, Achilles, Achoo," Stink read.

"Bless you," said Judy.

"No, that's a name: Achoo!"

"No way is somebody named Achoo," said Judy.

Stink frowned. "You're right. My star can't be named for a sneeze."

He flipped some pages. "Sheesh. There are ten hundred names in here. It will take light-years to find the right name."

"Close your eyes, open the book, and point," said Judy.

Stink closed his eyes. Stink opened the book. Stink pointed. "Lollipop,"

he read. "Ten thousand names and I point to the name of a big slobbery sucker?"

Stink went to find Mom and Dad. He asked them how to choose a brand-new, not-sneezy, un-slobbery-sucker name to put on a star.

"A name should say something about you," said Mom.

"Like Judy is moody? And Riley Rottenberger is rotten?" asked Stink.

"Sort of," said Dad.

"And like Stink is stinky?" said Judy.

"Try thinking of something that makes you special," said Dad. "Or someone you admire."

Stink's face lit up. "I got it! Albert Einstink!"

"Forget it, Stink Face," said Judy. "Your brain is way too puny."

"How about my initials and my birthday: JEM-229."

"My brother, the robot," said Judy.

"How about a super-cool spy name, like Mosquito? Or Neptune Shadow?"

"That's it!" said Judy.

"Really?"

"N-O!" said Judy. "Let's put all the names in a bowl, Stink. We'll mix them up. Then close your eyes, reach in, and pull one out."

"Hey! You just gave me an idea," said Stink. He scribbled in his notebook. "Ready for this?"

"Ready, Freddy!" said Judy. "Hercules-Balthazar-Superman-Dracula-Achoo-Lollipop-JEM-229-Mosquito-Albert-Einstink."

"You're going to name your star Hercules-Balthazar-Superman-Dracula-Achoo-Lollipop-JEM-229-Mosquito-Albert-Einstink?"

"Right."

HERCULES-BALTHAZAR-
SUPERMAN-DRACULA-
ACHOO-LOLLIPOP-
JEM-229-MOSQUITO-
ALBERT-EINSTINK

Judy picked up the way-official star packet. She read silently for about a hundred light-years. Then she said, "Stink, there are rules. First of all, a star name can't be more than sixteen letters long. The name you picked is like sixteen million letters long. Plus some numbers!"

"Yikes," said Stink.

"Second of all, a star name can only be one word. Your name is nine million words long."

"Double yikes," said Stink. He scratched his head.

"I know!" he said. "How about if my star's name is Hercules-Balthazar-Superman-Dracula-Achoo-Lollipop-JEM-229-Mosquito-Albert-Einstink, but you call it Stink for short?"

"Perfect," said Mom and Dad.

"You think?" asked Stink.

"If the Stink fits, wear it," said Judy.